# MY PAATI'S SARIS

written by
Jyoti Rajan
Gopal

illustrated by
Art Twink

Kokila

My paati's saris are stories.
They whisper the name
of where they were made and
how they came to be.

Peacocks preening,
lotus blooms peeking,
elephants parading—
my paati's saris call to me.

I can hide in their folds,
crisp cotton, shimmery silk, crinkly crepe.
I peep out
and see . . .

ME!
Wrapped in color.
Brilliant. Bold.
Cool. Quiet.
Muted tones murmur;
bright tones buzz.
My paati's saris speak to me.

My paati's pallu
holds sweet-smelling jasmine
and musky rose.

We thread the flowers,
a garland
for morning puja.
Paati tucks one behind
my ear.
A frangipani.

Walking to market,
I hold on tight
as shoppers jostle

and peddlers yell, selling
ripe mangoes, plump eggplants.
Laddoos and barfis
bursting with sweet spices
beg to be eaten.

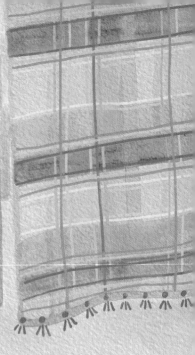

বনিক
জুয়েলার্স

But I stay close,
safe and sound,
by my paati's sari.

In her kitchen,
turmeric, cumin, and pepper
tickle my nose.
Pea pods snap,
mustard seeds crackle,
and sambar simmers,
savory, spicy.

Then . . .
incense, vibhuti, a whiff of marigold,
and it's time to celebrate.
As drummers drum
and dancers dance
and music plays,

my paati's sari SWIRLS.
Peacocks preening,
lotus blooms peeking,
elephants parading—
my paati's saris
SING to me.

The next morning . . .

draped and tucked,
pleated and folded,
pallu cascading
or cinched in tight,
my paati's saris invite me to
EXPLORE,
DARE,
BE.

I twirl
and sway . . .
They see me.
ME.

My paati's saris are
my shelter, my home.

From then to now,
from old to young,
a thread that weaves
through the years
and joins us,
a family.

My paati's saris are stories.
Stories of
my paati . . .
and me.